How Do I Show I Care?

Caring for Others

Rory McCallum

SOCIAL AND EMOTIONAL LEARNING FOR THE REAL WORLD™

Rosen Classroom™

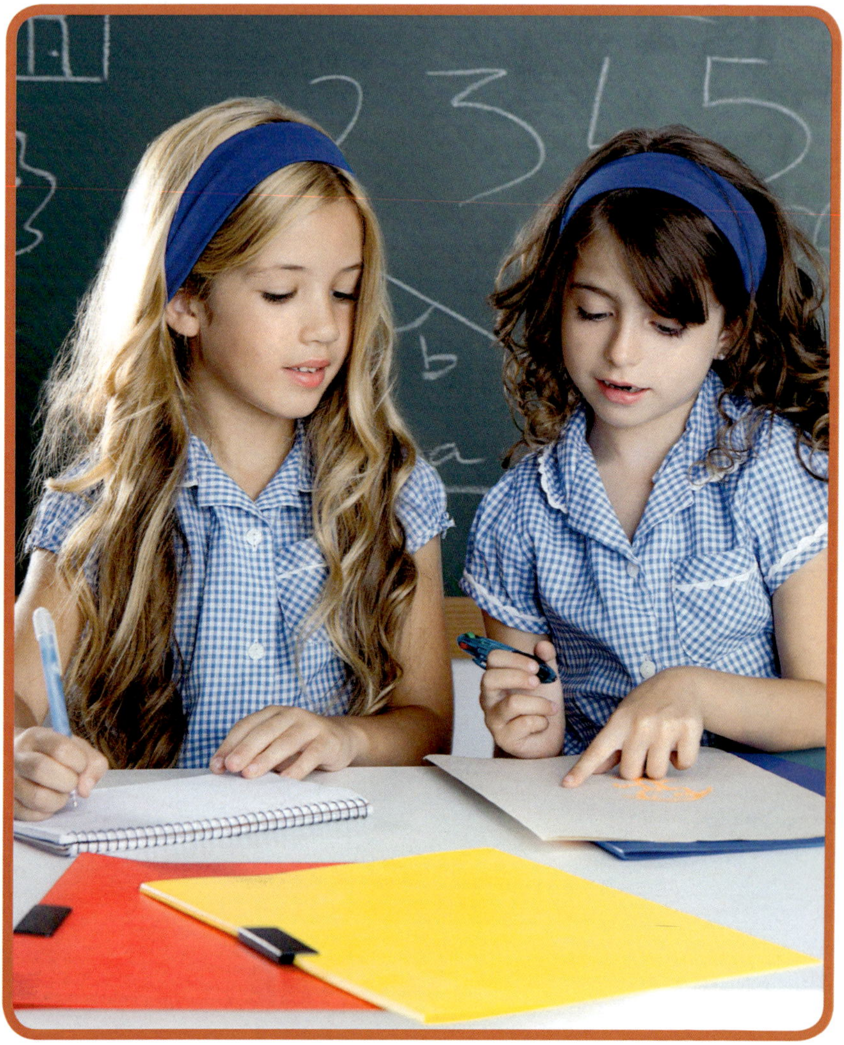

I care.

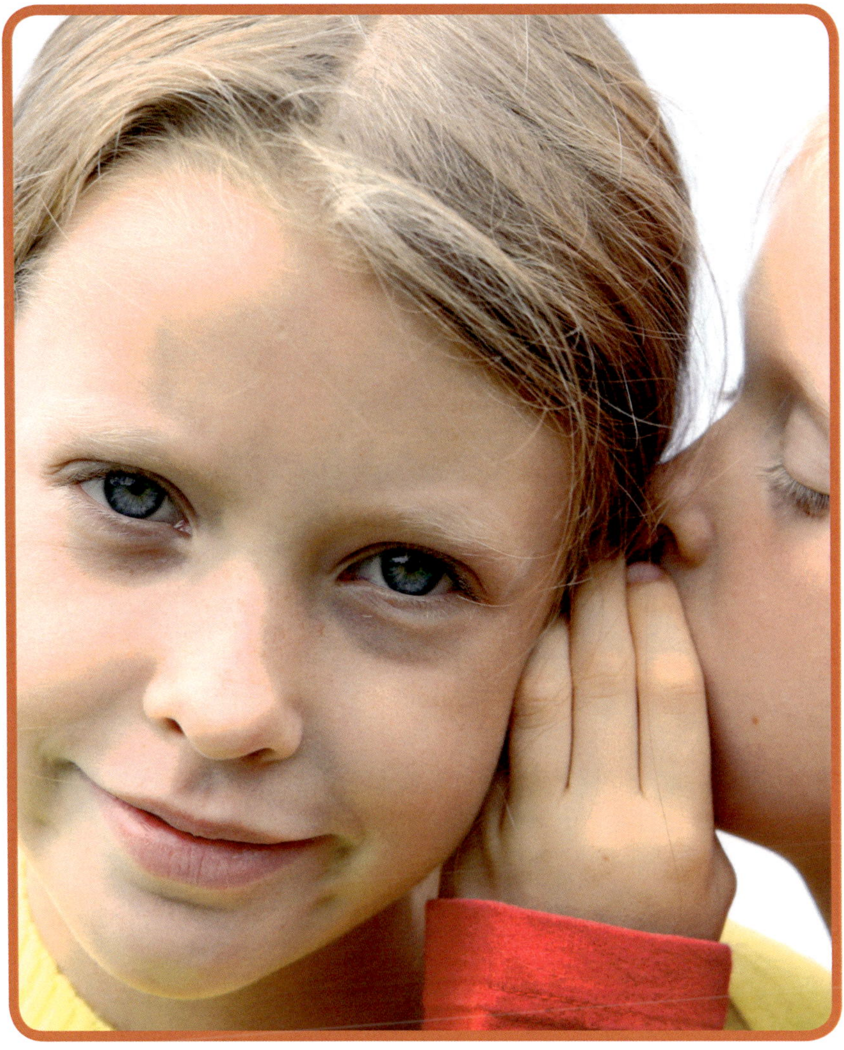

I listen.

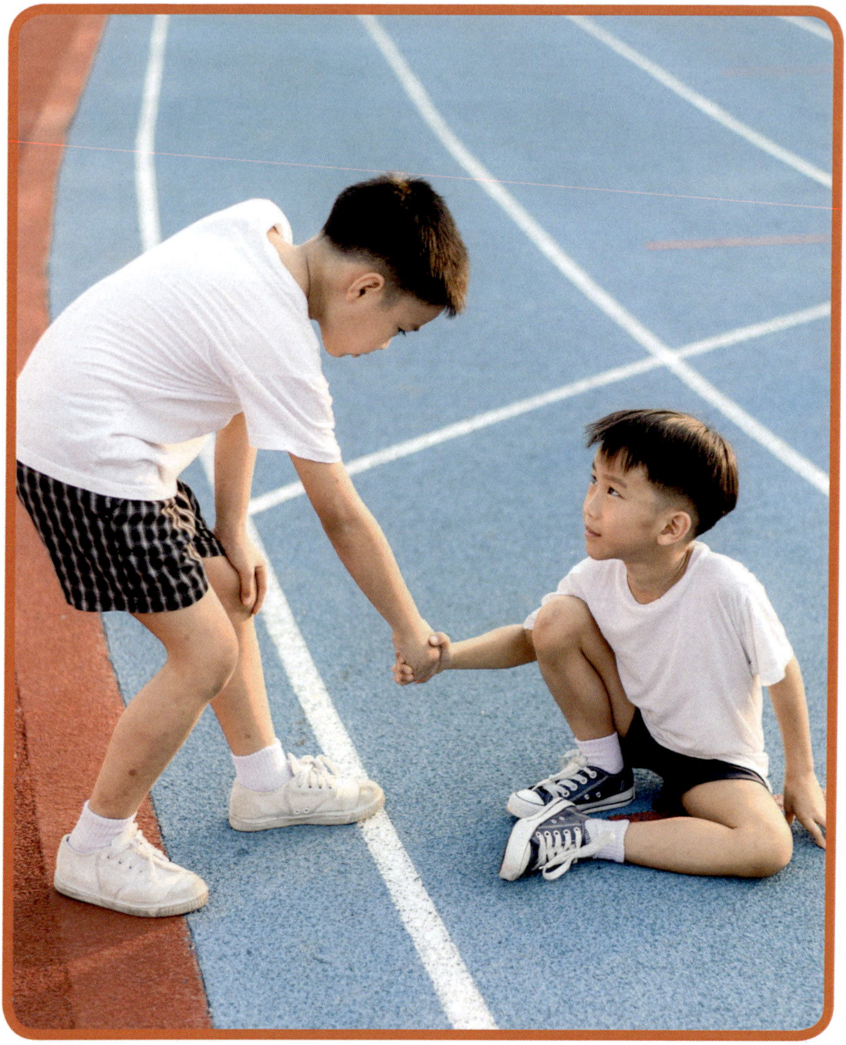

I help.

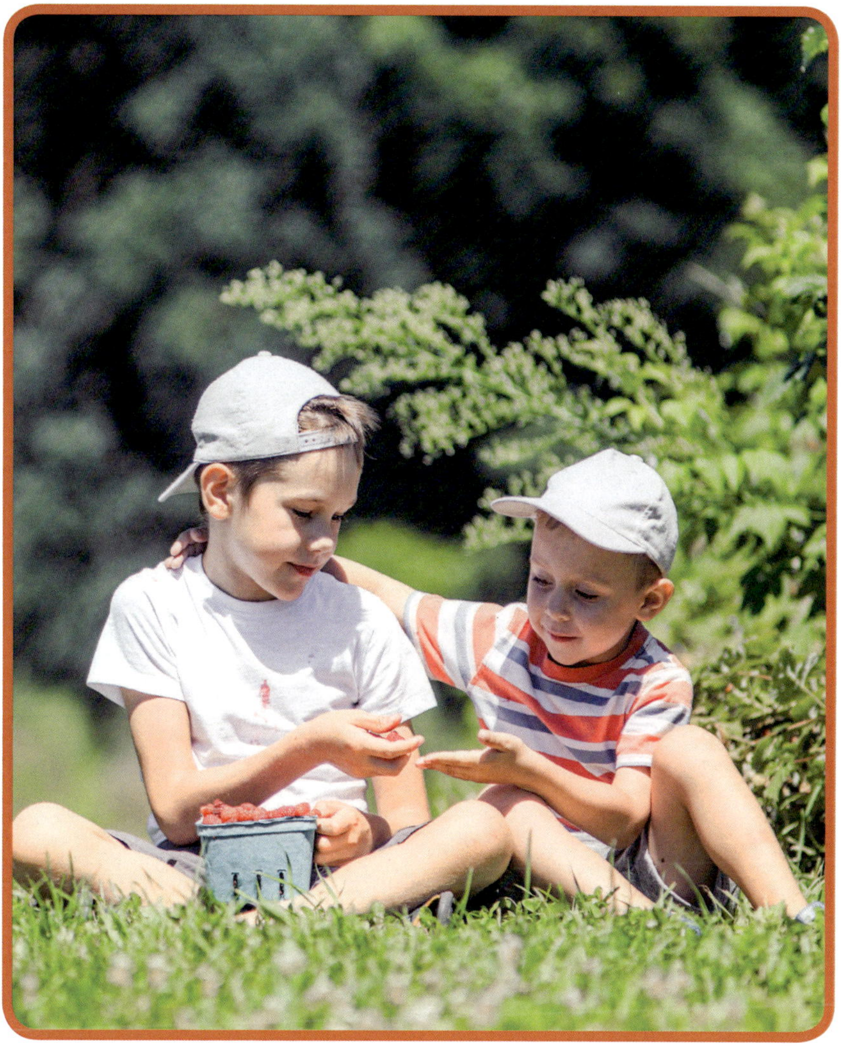

I share.

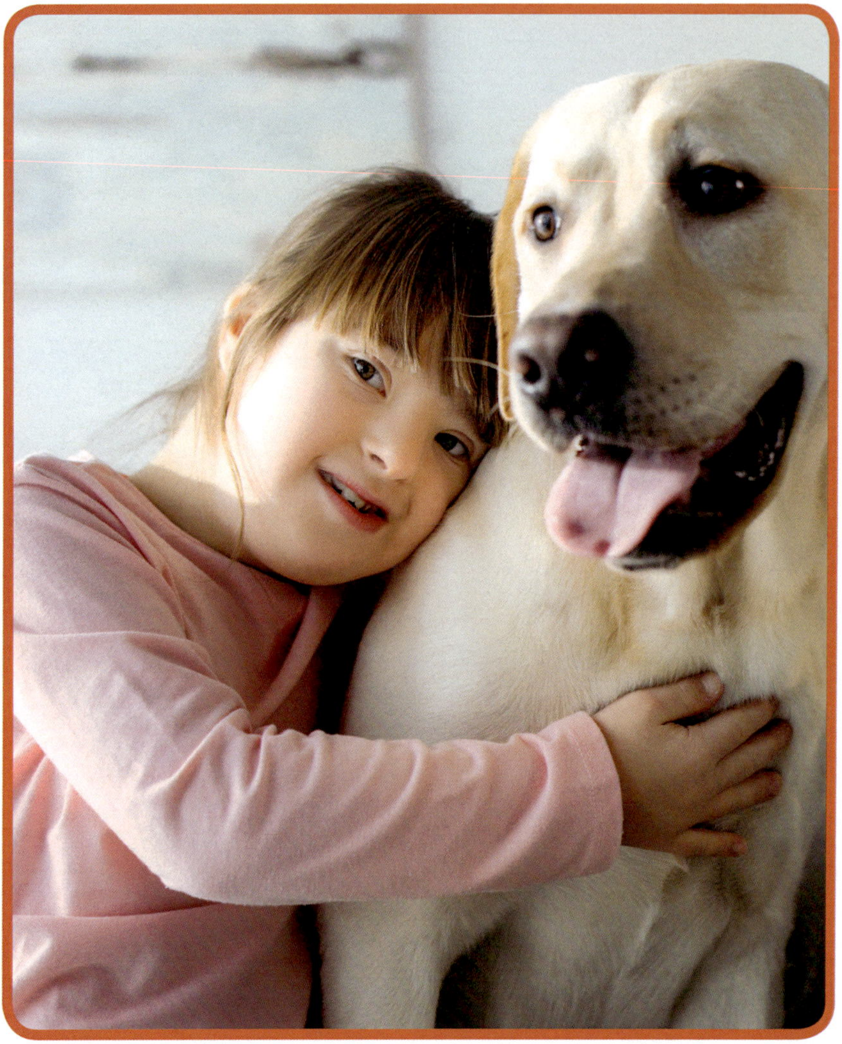

I pet.

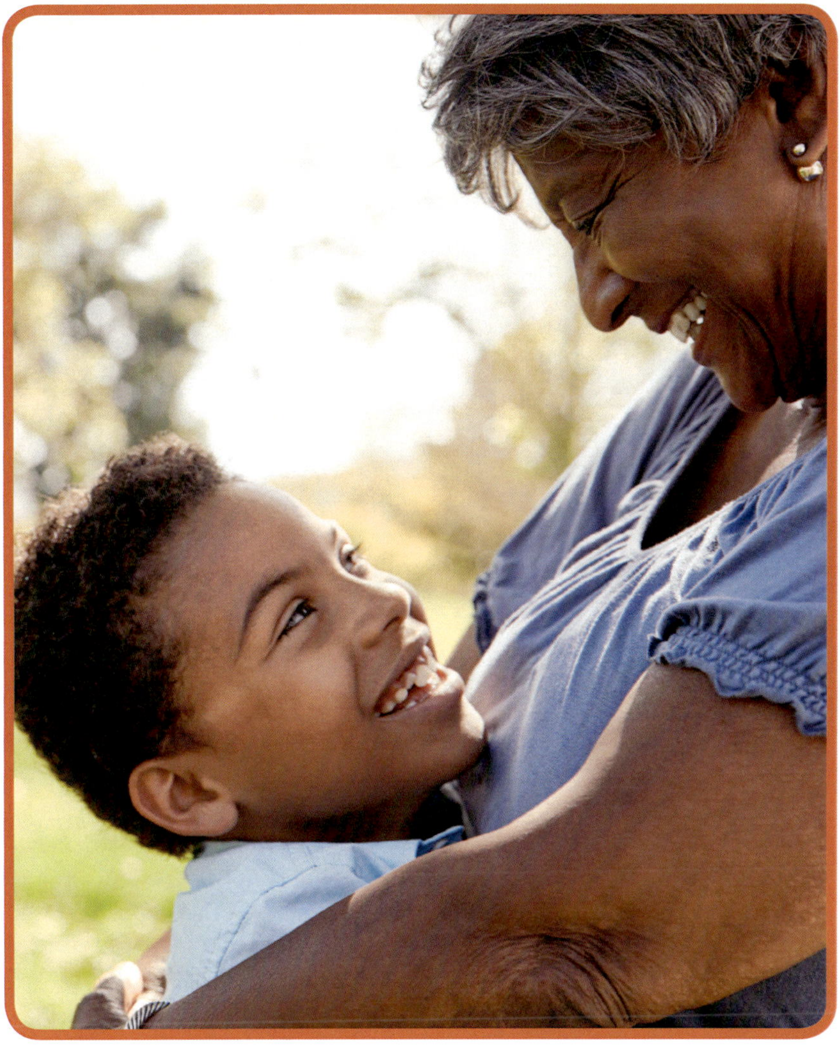

I hug.

Words to Know

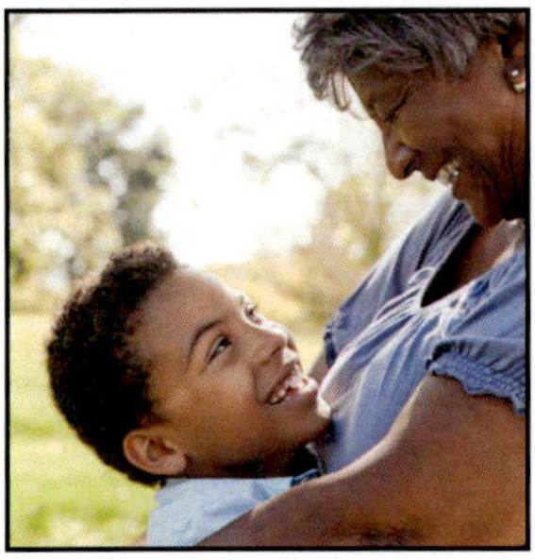

hug

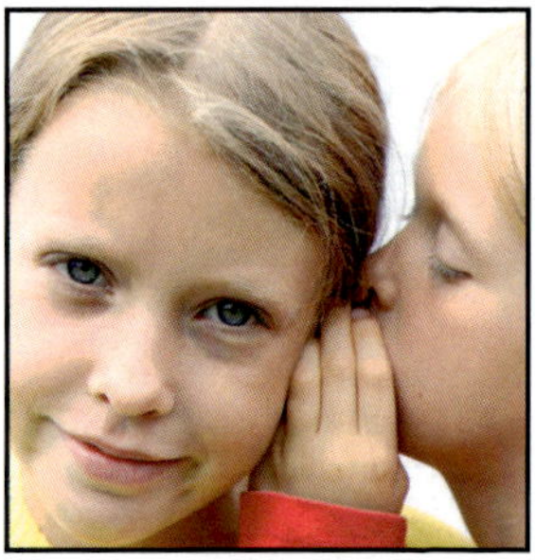

listen

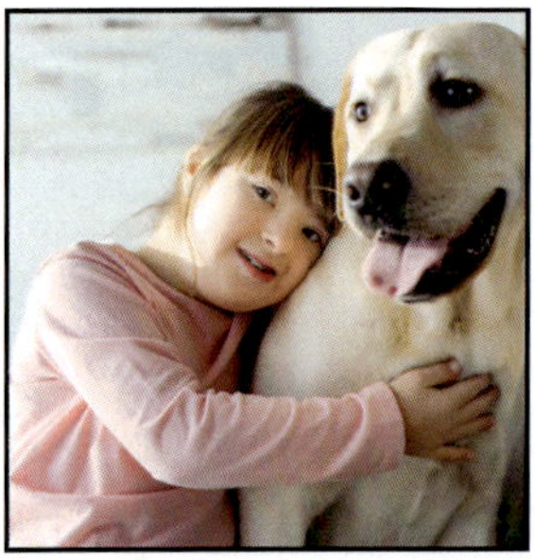

pet

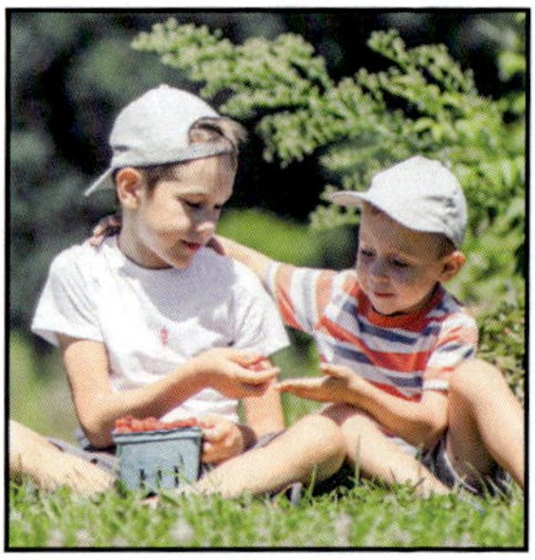

share